Dear Parents:

Congratulations! Your child is taking the first steps on an exciting journey. The destination? Independent reading!

STEP INTO READING® will help your child get there. The program offers five steps to reading success. Each step includes fun stories and colorful art or photographs. In addition to original fiction and books with favorite characters, there are Step into Reading Non-Fiction Readers, Phonics Readers and Boxed Sets, Sticker Readers, and Comic Readers—a complete literacy program with something to interest every child.

Learning to Read, Step by Step!

Ready to Read   Preschool–Kindergarten
• big type and easy words • rhyme and rhythm • picture clues
For children who know the alphabet and are eager to begin reading.

Reading with Help   Preschool–Grade 1
• basic vocabulary • short sentences • simple stories
For children who recognize familiar words and sound out new words with help.

Reading on Your Own   Grades 1–3
• engaging characters • easy-to-follow plots • popular topics
For children who are ready to read on their own.

Reading Paragraphs   Grades 2–3
• challenging vocabulary • short paragraphs • exciting stories
For newly independent readers who read simple sentences with confidence.

Ready for Chapters   Grades 2–4
• chapters • longer paragraphs • full-color art
For children who want to take the plunge into chapter books but still like colorful pictures.

STEP INTO READING® is designed to give every child a successful reading experience. The grade levels are only guides; children will progress through the steps at their own speed, developing confidence in their reading. The F&P Text Level on the back cover serves as another tool to help you choose the right book for your child.

Remember, a lifetime love of reading starts with a single step!

This book is dedicated to shiny, brilliant YOU!
May you find many magical ways to be awesome!
–M.R.R.

All rights reserved. Published in the United States by Random House Children's Books, a division of Penguin Random House LLC, New York.

Step into Reading, Random House, and the Random House colophon are registered trademarks of Penguin Random House LLC. HAPPY HAIR is a registered trademark of Happy Hair.

Visit us on the Web!
StepIntoReading.com
rhcbooks.com

Educators and librarians, for a variety of teaching tools, visit us at RHTeachersLibrarians.com

Library of Congress Cataloging-in-Publication Data
Name: Roe, Mechal Renee, author.
Title: I am born to be awesome! / written and illustrated by Mechal Renee Roe.
Description: First edition. | New York : Random House Children's Books, [2023] | Series: Step into reading | Audience: Ages 3–5. | Summary: "Illustrations and rhyming text reveal all of the things boys love, including music, nature, sports, and school." —Provided by publisher.
Identifiers: LCCN 2022012947 (print) | LCCN 2022012948 (ebook) |
ISBN 978-0-593-43321-8 (paperback) | ISBN 978-0-593-43322-5 (library binding) |
ISBN 978-0-593-43323-2 (ebook)
Subjects: CYAC: Stories in rhyme. | Likes and dislikes—Fiction. | Self-esteem—Fiction. |
LCGFT: Stories in rhyme. | Picture books.
Classification: LCC PZ8.3.R6185 Iam 2023 (print) | LCC PZ8.3.R6185 (ebook) | DDC [E]—dc23

Printed in the United States of America

10 9 8 7 6 5 4 3 2 1

This book has been officially leveled by using the F&P Text Level Gradient™ Leveling System.

I Am Born to be Awesome!

A HAPPY HAIR® BOOK

by Mechal Renee Roe

Random House 🏠 New York

I am born to be
awesome!

I love the stars!

I love racing

cars!

I love my beats!

I love to eat!

I am born to be awesome!

I love the trees!

I love the bees!

I love to bake!

I love to make

a cake!

I am born to be awesome!

I love to hop!

I love the barbershop!

I love the sand!

I love playing
in a band!

I am born to be awesome!

I love math!

I love to take

a bath!

I love to skip!

I love to flip!

I am born to be
awesome!

I love to float!

I love to sail
my boat!

I love the fall!

I love to play ball!

I am born to be awesome!

I love to rap!

I love my baseball cap!

I love my face!

I love winning
first place!

I am born to be awesome!

I love to spell!

I love show-and-tell!

I love to sing!

I love being a king!

What ways
are you awesome?